My Life in Smiley:
IT'S ALL GOOD

Acknowledgments

I'd like to thank Clémentine Sanchez for her meticulous help, Alexandra Bentz for her trust, Manon Soutreau and Samantha Thiery for their support and direction, as well as the entire Smiley team.

 For Lola, who always had a smile on her face.

my Life in SMILEY®

ANNE KALICKY

IT'S ALL GOOD

Andrews McMeel
PUBLISHING®

Warning to all
unwanted readers! !!

This work is authorized to be read only after

Friday, April 19, 2126.

If you have discovered this notebook before this date, do not open it! But if you're reading these words, then it means you already have. Your only hope is to close it immediately, or you'll seriously regret it . . . especially if your names are Dad, Mom, Lisa, Marion, or Raoul! Beware: I have placed a curse on the following pages. If you don't heed this warning, your eyes will burn and turn neon yellow. Your hands will sprout enormous black blisters that shoot out hundreds of spiders (tarantulas, to be exact). If you have the bad idea (which I bet you would) to pick your nose and then put your fingers in your mouth to eat the boogers, your tongue will triple in size and disintegrate so you can never tell anyone what you've just read.

Close this notebook immediately . . . or you are certain to die a horrible death!

Dear future human,

You who were forced to leave Earth to migrate to a distant planet, this masterpiece is for **YOU**. Because, let's be clear: this notebook is not a diary, OK? It is an autobiographical masterpiece: that of a true hero from a bygone era. I am writing for a noble cause—for the future. No other reason!

 Actually, to fill you in quickly, I just saw a weird show on TV that was talking about a planet called Eratosthenes that seemed oddly similar to Earth. The beginning of the show was really interesting. Scientists described the possibility of living on this new planet one day. But then it went downhill: humans had to quickly evacuate to go live on Eratosthenes because the Earth's atmosphere had suddenly become unbreathable!

So after seeing this show, I asked myself, "What if that really happens? What will I have done for the coming generations?" I then had this great idea to write about the big steps of my life so I can become a true hero. In four days, for example, I'll start middle school. There you have it—a big milestone!

SO IT'S NOW OR NEVER TO GIVE IT A TRY!

One day, I'm sure, someone will discover my memoirs in the safe of an abandoned space shuttle, and I'LL MAKE IT INTO HISTORY WITH A CAPITAL H.

Dear future human,

While waiting to go back to school, I'll take the opportunity to tell you a little about myself. My name is Maxime, and I live in France. OK, would've rather been named Bruce or Clark. . . .

so I

Luckily, everyone calls me Max—nicknames are way cooler. I'm eleven years old, and I have two sisters: Lisa is eight, but she's still my parents' little baby. And Marion, she's fourteen, and she's so annoyyyyyyying!

Even on Eratosthenes, she'd be sent back to Earth for being so annoyyyyyyying! Maybe you future people are lucky enough to have parents who took some kind of a cyber-pill to give you a little brother instead.

Unfortunately for me, that isn't the case:
I'm surrounded by girls, and for that alone I
should be awarded a medal.

The proof? I looked in the dictionary and
"SISTER" rhymes with:

BLISTER

TWISTER

LISTERine

(OK, so that last one
is a stretch. . . .)

THINGS ARE
GOING
SWIMMINGLY!

My parents are
kind of lame, or
uncool at the very least,
but overall, they're OK.
My dad works at S Inc.,
a company that makes
sinks.

My mom works in a laboratory, but I've never really understood what she does exactly. Oh! Oh! Dear future human, want to know my parents' favorite joke?

Have a good think, my dear!

Have a good sink, my dear!

I live in a house in the suburbs. Sometimes it gets a little boring. But I often go on vacation to the countryside in Brittany to stay with Grandpa Joff and Grandma Ragny. Yeah . . . I know what you're thinking, future human—there's nothing surprising or exciting in my everyday, mundane life . . . but wait till you read the rest of my work. ⟶

TOM MARTIN is my neighbor and best bud. He's also been in my class since kindergarten. He's a real nerd, he's super skinny, he wears glasses, and he knows TONS of stuff—like how to make <u>invisible ink with yogurt</u> or even a <u>volcanic eruption using carrot juice</u>. He always gets good grades. My dad always says you should have friends who are better than you. But I already knew that.

TOM AND MAX'S FIVE BEST ADVENTURES:

☑ LONG-DISTANCE PEEING COMPETITION

☑ REACHING THE **NINTH** LEVEL OF *ZOMBIELAND* ON XBOX

☑ NOT SHOWERING FOR A WHOLE WEEK

☑ CHICKEN NUGGET EATING RECORD: **TWENTY-THREE EACH!**

☑ SPYING ON GIRLS IN THE BATHROOM

Dear future human, **Wednesday**

This morning I started sixth grade. I was so excited! I've wanted to go to middle school since the first grade, for three reasons:

FIRST

I get to go to school by myself, and I can finally escape my parents yelling, "Give me a kiss, Maxie-poo."

SECOND I get a cell phone.

THIRD

 I'm officially a <u>TEENAGER!</u> Ultra cool!

But I fell victim to the cruel reality that adolescence isn't cool AT ALL! 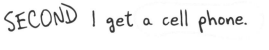 OK, so I do have a cell phone—my mom's old phone programmed for "minimum apps, maximum supervision" mode.

Then, for the first day, my mom bought me really dorky clothes: Bermuda shorts and a navy-blue polo shirt. I still wore them . . . but only to make her happy. When I found Tom on the way to school, he looked even worse: he had on tan pants that were way too big for him and a pink checkered short-sleeve shirt. We walked together, but we didn't talk much. When we finally reached the schoolyard, both of us immediately regretted not going back home to change our clothes—or, better yet, being held back for another year in elementary school. I realized pretty quickly, seeing the other students who were five heads taller than me, that I was now one of the little kids. I even heard a big, tough ninth-grader say, "Oh, hey, there's the class of dwarves!" Tom and I checked the bulletin board to find that we were in the same class. Phew! That was some good news!

The bad news . . . our homeroom teacher is Mr. Schmitt, the English teacher. 😐 He's weird: he taps his foot all the time on the desk. I think that he's actually afraid of students. In five hundred years, maybe teachers will be replaced by robots. WHAT LUCK! In the classroom there were little labels on the tables. Mr. Schmitt had already assigned us seats. And guess who I found myself sitting next to? RAOUL KADOR!

He spent the entire morning sticking his boogers on Maud's chair in front of him.

Thinks he's hot stuff. Spikes his hair with tons of gel

Reeks of body spray

Fake tattoos he makes with gum wrappers

MATTHIS BALMA   RAOUL KADOR   DAMIEN CHICO   LUCAS SAILLARD

His gang of big losers

There's no point in trying to get along with these morons. Mr. Schmitt gave everyone our class schedule and made us fill out registration forms: last name, first name, birthday, parents' jobs, and what we want to be when we grow up. "FUTURE GENIUS," I wrote. OK, so I may have set the bar a little bit high.

Tom and I decided to meet up every day to walk to school together. We found a trick to get there quicker and avoid running into Raoul Kador and his gang of losers: we go through the "secret passage." NO ONE but us knows about it. OK, I'm exaggerating a bit! It's really just a shortcut . . . a little street with a building on one side and a big wall on the other. Behind the wall there's an empty lot, I think. I've never really taken a close look over there. On the wall, there's a big spray paint inscription.

Friday

Dear future human,

After a pretty quiet week, today was the <u>WORST day of my life!</u> (◉◡◉) This morning it was impossible to get up. First my mom came in to give me a hug, and then she left for work.

Later my dad came and knocked on the door and yelled something in Russian.

EEYA NYE GAVARDYU OCHEN RALACHO PARUSKI!

I didn't understand a thing. (◕︵◕)

I thought that it might mean, "Get up, little lazybones, it's time!" but my dad explained to me later that it only meant, "I do not speak Russian very well. . . . " (He's been taking Russian classes for work for a few months. He doesn't seem to be studying a lot. . . .) Then after about ten minutes, Marion came to tell me I had five minutes left before she was leaving for school without me.

14

It was basically my last chance to arrive on time, because I'd missed my rendezvous with Tom. Going with Marion is always my last resort.

SHE'S SO ANNOYYYYYING!!!

That definitely woke me up. I jumped into my tennis shoes, jeans, and sweatshirt. I grabbed my backpack and took off for school.

I had math, French, and English in the morning.
During recess I played marbles and lost five in
the sewer drain. I noticed Célia and Naïs doing
each other's hair. . . . Naïs is pretty,
but her new hairstyle
was kind of strange.

In the lunchroom, they were serving
some unidentifiable vegetables. Anyway, it was
after lunch that my day really became a MESS.
We had gym, and (of course) since I wasn't
really awake this morning, I'd forgotten my gym
clothes. But the worst came when I realized in
the bathroom, about ten minutes before the start
of class, that not only did I forget my sweatpants
but I had my pajama bottoms on
under my jeans! And not the really
cool soccer bottoms with Pietro on
them, oh no!

My life is so unfair. I <u>ALWAYS</u> get
Marion's little pajamas. . . . Long
story short, what you need to know is that
Mr. Ramoupoulos is <u>DEFINITELY</u> a tracksuit
psycho!! (Mr. Ramoupoulos is the gym teacher,
he's Greek, and he has two quirks: when he's
happy, his nostrils twitch, and he wears nothing
but tracksuits!) I immediately thought about last
year when a student—who wishes to remain
anonymous—had his sports bag eaten by
a mangy stray dog. . . .

Well, at least that was his excuse. He then went to gym class wearing jeans, but he wore them really saggy . . . like a rapper. Mr. Ramoupoulos told him that because he was trying to show everyone his underwear, he didn't need his jeans. . . . Jérémy (Oops! I said it! ) had to run ten times around the track in his boxers . . . HORRIBLE! In short, I had a flying saucer problem—I had to make sure that NO ONE saw them. Not Mr. Ramoupoulos, not anyone in the bleachers, and nobody in the locker room! Otherwise, it would be guaranteed embarrassment!

All of this is Marion's fault: my vengeance will be FIERCE!!!

PEPPER

MARION'S MAKEUP

I came up with three possible solutions:

 One, I could hide in the bathroom and skip gym class (but risk dying alone, cruelly asphyxiated by the infamous odor that dominates that part of the school).

 Two, I could go in pajamas and claim that during the night, Martians had chosen me as an experimental subject (which could maybe make me a hero in the eyes of Naïs).

Or, three, I could go talk to Tom, who always has great ideas.

After thinking about my horrible predicament for way too long, I realized I had only five minutes left. Temporarily renouncing the idea of becoming a hero, I got dressed at top speed and went to see Tom. He was crouched behind the school garden in the middle of running a three-snail race. I told him everything.

EVEN THE SNAILS LAUGHED!

After a never-ending silence, his response was as slow as his little mollusks.

"Just go look in the lost 'n' found—there might be a pair of old sweats in there."

This guy was a genius! 😄 I rushed across the playground and searched in the bin, and there miraculously waiting for me was a pair of red sweatpants! They went perfectly with my . . . yellow shirt. I could already hear Raoul calling me a red and yellow pepper salad, but that was a lot better than looking like I'd just rolled out of bed. I had only two minutes to spare. I went back to the bathroom, I took off my clothes and pajamas, and I hid them behind a pipe. The bell rang, and I threw on the sweatpants. . . . I arrived a little late to class, but I was already dressed, so I was ready before everyone else. Mr. Ramoupoulos even congratulated me on being prompt—at least I think so. I'm sure I saw his nostrils twitch.

Phew! I was scared!
Tom saved my life today!

Before going home I discreetly returned the sweatpants to where I found them, and I put the spaceship pajamas back on, but shhh! Don't tell my mom—it's a secret.

Saturday

I dreamt that I was kidnapped by Martians who wanted to steal my pajamas. Their leader, Mr. Ramoupoulos, was all green with antennae on his head, big bulbous eyes, and, of course, gigantic nostrils. He commanded me in Russian to get into his spaceship by climbing up a smooth rope. I was giving it my all, but I couldn't even get above the knot. The more I tried to climb, the more tangled I became in the rope. The spaceship, driven by Ramoupoulos, carried me into the air,

 tied up like a sausage. I yelled, "Let me down! Let me down!"

When I woke up, it was six in the morning. I couldn't go back to sleep. I think all of this talk about extraterrestrials and the unknown planet is getting inside my head! But what more do you want, dear future human—that's what heroes dream about!

22

HUGE SCAM at school!

Today at the beginning of social studies class with Mr. Boulfou, the principal came and told our class that we'd been chosen by the city for a field trip. We all cheered. But that was BEFORE he told us what the field trip was: "We are exceedingly pleased to give you the opportunity to create and perform a show in honor of Pleasant Gardens!" When you realize that "Pleasant Gardens" is the name for a RETIREMENT HOME, you understand why the principal was talking about us "doing a good deed."

The blending of generations is the beginning of a better world.

Afterward, he told us that the people in the old folks' home were preparing surprises for us and, in exchange, we were going to have to practice a song with Mr. Boulfou every Wednesday until fall break. The song is called "Hope and Life." The principal left, and Mr. Boulfou just couldn't wait until Wednesday. He asked for a volunteer to sing the refrain as a solo. Raoul Kador leaned over, pretending to pick up a crayon. He pinched me, and I yelled. The teacher thought I was volunteering and . . . the soloist chosen . . . was ME!

ME!.

Before I could defend myself, the stereo suddenly started playing, and it let out such a terrible crackle that I thought sparks would burst out of the speakers. I crossed my fingers and hoped the teacher would start a fire. But the melody of a violin began playing at the same time as the croaky voice of Mr. Boulfou.

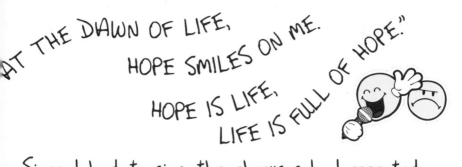

"AT THE DAWN OF LIFE, HOPE SMILES ON ME. HOPE IS LIFE, LIFE IS FULL OF HOPE."

Since I had to sing the chorus solo, I repeated the words after the teacher. I had a huge lump stuck in my throat from the humiliation. Tom, he had a runny nose. At first I thought he was crying because of the lyrics, but actually it was just because the classroom was really cold. The song is totally stupid.

Besides that episode, Tom and I went through the secret passage on our way home, and the message on the wall had changed.

It's strange; I get the feeling that these messages are for me. . . .

Wednesday

Dear future human,

After recess, we ALL practiced with Mr. Boulfou, and I sang the refrain ALL ALONE. And, of course, Raoul died laughing. It's so embarrassing! I've got to find a way to get out of this field trip. After school, I asked Tom if he wanted to come to my house to finish *Zombieland* on the Xbox. I only had two more worlds left before I beat the last level. And Tom just HAD to witness my crushing victory! That video game is awesome. It's about the undead that rise from their graves to invade the Earth. The players have to fight the zombies with canned food. The more zombies you take out, the more points you win in order to advance to the next level. And I am SOOO GOOD at it!

When we got to my house, I heated up some leftover pasta in the microwave. Tom slopped a ton of mayonnaise on his pasta while humming "Hope and Life" the entire time. AS SOON as I started the game, Marion and her two friends showed up! Since I'm not allowed to play video games during the week, you can be sure she was going to jump at the chance to rat me out to our parents! 😦 They went straight to the bathroom and closed the door, but the peace didn't last. A quarter of a second later Marion came out to <u>bug me.</u>

She always has to bring up something in front of her friends to make herself seem important!

SHE IS SO ANOOOOOYYYYYYYIIIIING!!!

She slammed the bathroom door. I decided to ignore her—it was game on, and I was going to demolish Tom! 🙁 But no! My sister and her friends came out of the bathroom to go into Marion's room. Wham! Slamming the door again. I jumped so high that I lost the game, just at the very second when I was going to squash the zombie boss. That was too much for me! I got up and went to her room, ready to scream at my sister, when I saw that all of the girls' faces were caked with makeup.

Raccoon eyes

Phosphorescent red lips

Duckface

I asked them what they were doing. They told me that they were taking "selfies," then they slammed the door in my face. Girls can be so stupid! 🧠 The door closed before I could even ask, "What are selfies?" I went back to ask Tom. He's a walking dictionary. But he didn't seem to know this time, given his fishy expression. While waiting to figure out what the girls had meant, he had time to steal my controller and was focused on his turn. I went over to my dad's computer. I know his password—too easy: it's Lisa! 😁 I looked up:

SELFIE 🔍

MAX

1

Wikipedia told me that they're "self-portraits" that are often distributed on social media.

Dear future human, if you are in possession of these kinds of portraits from the twenty-first century, know that they are not works of art, OK? Don't bother selling them at big art shows with dreams of becoming a millionaire; they aren't worth A THING! Especially those of my sister and her friends! Anyway, I'd have my revenge: if Marion told my parents I was playing video games during the week, I'd tell them she was posting pictures online of herself with too much makeup.

MARION

GAME OVER

I went back to confront her and put my blackmail plan into action. But when I went in, they were all sitting on the floor reading their history books. I still tried to bug my sister, who was more than happy to show me that her phone only had pictures of last summer with Grandpa Joff and Grandma Ragny. Then she told me to "beat it." I stayed there and watched them through the keyhole to catch them in the act, but . . . nothing—they continued to pretend they were "studying."

In the evening, Marion snitched that I had played video games all afternoon with Tom; I didn't know what to say in my defense.

DA HZDV HHCAZD GMONZADJHB!!

When I went to bed, I opened my phone, and what did I find?

When I was spying on my sister, that wimp Tom had seized the opportunity to take selfies with my phone.

Dear future human,

Tonight at dinner, Lisa said that her teacher is allowing them to do presentations this year. My parents were very impressed. Hmph! Lisa is always their favorite.

"Super! What a great idea! That's wonderful!" my dad said.

"What are you going to do your presentation on? The pyramids? Volcanoes?" asked my mom.

"No, Romane and I are going to do a presentation on Ben Didji." ⟶

Ben Didji is Lisa's idol. Last year, this heart-melting idiot won a reality TV show called *The Choice.* All summer it was *The Choice* or nothing. One time my mom took her to an autograph session at the supermarket close to our house. Lisa begged me to come along too. We waited in line three hours to see him for about three seconds. I had to hide the entire time we were waiting. I kept imagining Raoul Kador showing up and torturing me in line.

I also found it a bit unfair that her teacher would let them do a presentation on their idol instead of on a more cultural subject. I, for instance, would have loved to do a project on Pietro, my favorite soccer player.

Anyway, Lisa showed us what she'd started to sketch for her presentation:

♡ *Presentation on Ben Didji* ♡

Ben iz an singer vere young (18 years old). His birday iz Mae 10th. He win *The Choice* on his birday (the 10th of Mae). He is singel (He doesn't have a wive).

OK, I've made a decision: I've got to find a way out of this field trip to the retirement home. It isn't that I doubt my ability to sing in front an "undoubtedly" appreciative audience, but this sort of performance is beneath me.

Dear future human,

I dreamt the entire night that I was a rock star performing at a concert and Raoul was in the front row. He was screaming, "Max Didjiiiii, Max Didjiiii!" Forget it—it was a

 NIGHTMARE!!!

This morning we had PE with Mr. Ramoupoulos. In the gym there were mats spread around with all sorts of torture devices. I sensed that the next two hours weren't exactly going to be a picnic. The teacher told us that we were going to begin "rhythmic gymnastics," and he twitched his nostrils.

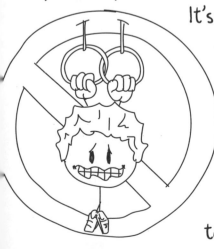 It's not exactly my strong suit. Personally, I'm better at team sports: soccer, basketball, dodgeball, Zombieland, etc. So you can imagine I found his announcement totally delightful.

Next, he passed out a paper with drawings of a guy doing a series of movements.

I felt my stomach sink. Mr. Ramoupoulos told us how to do the exercises, all the while remaining seated on his bench. I don't know how it is for you, future human, but in our times, gym teachers are always ready and willing to EXPLAIN how to do a backward somersault but rarely actually DO it.

When it was my turn, I perfectly executed a forward roll. On the other hand, when I did a backward roll, I got stuck with my butt in the air. As my head was upside down, I didn't know exactly where I was or how I could get out of this mess. And since everyone was in front of me, I didn't have anyone to help me.

Help! Someone help me!

It was a good five minutes before the teacher noticed that I was just on the verge of dying because my face was all red and I couldn't breathe.

Mr. Ramoupoulos blew his whistle, but that wasn't enough to untangle me, so he actually got up. He pushed me so I could finish my backward roll and then sat back down without giving me much technical advice on how to avoid this sort of incident in the future. 😠 That was the first exercise. Then, our group had to run on a mat, jump on a trampoline, land on the pommel horse, do push-ups, and then finish on a big foam mat (that reeked of dirty socks 😖). Dear future human, know that my century is BARBARIC. Forcing poor innocents like us to experience this sort of torment is a crime against humanity.

WANTED

RAMOUPOULOS

38

From afar, I could see that Naïs's group didn't fare too badly. I knew in advance that it was a lost cause, but I gathered what strength I had and launched myself with heroism. I sprinted, jumped on the trampoline, and . . . hopelessly missed the pommel horse before crumpling up on the big mat. A painful, predictable failure!

I came out unscathed, unlike Chloe, who had completely broken her shoulder last year. Her arm was all twisted, and it started swelling weirdly for the rest of the day. Still, the teacher had told her it was nothing and it would go away. Result: two months in a cast. I was unscathed . . . well . . . unfortunately, because while thinking of Chloe's twisted arm, I told myself that a really good injury with firemen and paramedics could have the added bonus of getting me out of the retirement home—I mean field trip. In the locker room, Raoul, who didn't miss my accident on the pommel horse, didn't deprive me of insults.

Monday

The field trip to the retirement home is rapidly approaching—it's next Friday. I have to do EVERYTHING in my power to GET SICK.

PLAN (A)

Methodically forget my coat so I can catch a cold.

PLAN (B)

Locate all sick students and
try to get their germs.

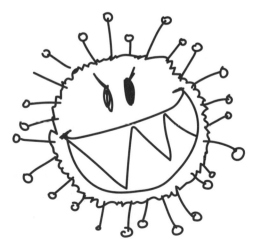

As it so happens, Theo's seat was empty this morning. Right away, I asked Mrs. Boulet, the French teacher, if I could take his homework to him. All day I demonstrated my extreme helpfulness as I took detailed notes for Theo.

 But when I stopped by his house after school, Theo told me he'd been at a funeral for his great-grandmother in Normandy. I felt sorry for him and all, but I was also really disappointed. Not only was he not sick but also he got to breathe fresh sea air the entire weekend: no chance he was getting sick in the next few days.

Yesterday, Raoul bragged during recess that he'd eaten an <u>entire box</u> of expired cereal in order to test his stamina, but then he complained about his upset stomach all throughout math class with Mr. Tamisole. When he got up to go to the bathroom, I realized: a stomachache would be the perfect excuse to get out of visiting the old folks' home and singing that ridiculous song! Since Raoul sits by me in class, and I spend close to six hours a day next to him, this was my lucky break (I would've loved to have made fun of him in front of everyone for the cereal incident— too bad this time). I saw him chew on his pen before putting it back in his pencil box. So, very discreetly, I stole the pen and bit on it myself. A bit disgusting, I know, but desperate times call for desperate measures.

To increase my chances of convincing Mr. Boulfou I wasn't the best person for a solo, I pretended to forget all of the words during practice:

AT THE END OF LIFE,
    THERE'S NO HOPE—YOU'RE THROUGH,
  BUT THE DOORS OF HEAVEN
          SMILE AT YOU . . .

You see, dear future human, I've got a knack for changing lyrics! But Mr. Boulfou didn't quite seem to appreciate it . . . at all.

Uhh . . . which refrain?

You will recopy the refrain fifty times in your notebook!

Tonight I told my mom I was beginning to have an upset stomach because Raoul ate an entire box of expired cereal. However, she then explained to me that indigestion isn't something you can catch.

This afternoon Lisa was scribbling on my hands, and it gave me a brilliant idea. I asked her if she could do me a little favor. . . .

The chickenpox marks looked great, even if I did have to add a few personal touches. In order to guarantee Lisa's silence, I promised her a gift. When my mom came home, I started acting sick and showed her my arms. She said it looked really serious. Then I told her I didn't know if I was going to be able to eat dinner and that I needed to go lie down. To make me feel better she pulled a bottle of special shower gel out of her bag.

47

I was SOO happy! 😃 I'd wanted it for weeks. I ran directly into the bathroom, 😁 I scrubbed up, and it smelled so good. For once I was actually happy to take a shower . . .

SHOWER GEL

. . . but I'd completely forgotten about my fake chickenpox. . . .

🙁

This morning I had to come to terms with the cold, hard truth: I was going to have to overcome the unavoidable humiliation and sing that HORRIBLE song before the entire class and a bunch of strangers. The only upside was that I escaped Mr. Ramoupoulos's gymnastics gauntlet. I found Tom on the way to school and explained my dilemma, hoping he'd offer a solution. He had plenty of ideas:

💡 Break an arm or a leg

💡 Eat some rocks

💡 Bump into a hornet's nest

He was on a roll, but I had to pump the brakes. He could see I still had a strange look on my face, and he wanted to cheer me up:

—"Do you know the joke about breakfast?"

—"No."

—"Well, I guess you're out of Lucky Charms then!"

That morning when we arrived at the bus for the field trip, Raoul and his clique of losers were already sitting in the best seats at the back.

We sat a couple of rows up, just behind Enzo Danleau—the biggest kid in our class. His mother had made him a tuna sandwich because Enzo hadn't had the time to eat breakfast that morning and also because it was Friday; at the Danleau house on Friday it's fish or nothing. He ate it right away. His mother had also prepared an apple pie for the people at the retirement home, which he held on his lap.

The bus started. After about ten minutes, Enzo started to feel carsick. After fifteen minutes, he barfed the tuna sandwich right on the apple pie and immediately started crying. Mr. Boulfou had to stop the bus to clean it all up. But it was too late: the bus already smelled disgusting. It was horrible! Then he moved Enzo all the way up front so that he could see the road, and we took off again.

To distract us, the teacher started playing "Hope and Life" on the radio. At the back of the bus, I saw Raoul pointing his finger at me and whispering, "Shout-out to Max!" In front, the teacher was standing up, gesturing wildly.

I was wondering if Enzo was about to toss his cookies again, but then I heard the driver ask Mr. Boulfou to sit down and respect the bus safety rules. The teacher didn't dare say a word for the rest of the trip.

Right when we arrived, I summoned up all my courage to take charge of my situation. I went to Mr. Boulfou and told him that I felt carsick too, that I didn't feel well at all, and that I was too queasy to sing. It was <u>ALMOST</u> true, I swear. But instead he just gave me some mints. <u>This time I was done for.</u>

The director of the retirement home greeted us with a pat on the head, as if we were four-year-olds. Then he took us to the main room where people who looked like Grandpa Joff and Grandma Ragny were waiting. They seemed nice, but it also looked like they'd been sitting there for years, which they probably had.

"Are you going to sing a round? I love rounds—it reminds me of my youth. . . ."

They had prepared cake, fruit juice, and milk for us. They'd also hung up a banner with different-colored letters:

WELCOME, KIDS!

They must've been expecting a class of first-graders to get off the bus.

Mr. Boulfou started getting frustrated because he wanted us to sing right away. Enzo's throw-up incident had thrown off the whole schedule. Personally, I wasn't in a hurry. He asked us to stand in front of the audience, and, while rummaging in his big sack, he told me to step forward one step with each refrain. Suddenly, he took out some heart-shaped hats and one in the shape of a sun. Evidently, the sun was for me, but the hearts were for everyone else. That made me feel a little bit better, because at least I wouldn't be the only one who looked ridiculous.

Raoul turned beet red, infuriated by the idea of wearing a heart on his head. Tom volunteered to pass out the hats.

Mr. Boulfou slid his CD in the room's stereo system. He turned toward us—his arms raised high, ready to lead like a conductor—and then it didn't work.

The director stepped in to see what was wrong, and they spent a half hour on all fours in front of all those wires (and we got to take off our hats). Out in the room, I saw a little old woman in a wheelchair who was talking to herself in front of the mirror.

I told myself that at least there'd be one person I didn't feel embarrassed in front of and that when I began singing, I'd focus on her. My dad always says the trick to public speaking is to look at one specific person. I thought that, for once, maybe he wasn't wrong.

Seeing as my dignity was about to be lost forever, it couldn't hurt to try his method. Finally, the music started ringing throughout the room, we put our hats back on, and we started to sing.

AT THE DAWN OF LIFE,
HOPE SMILES ON ME.
HOPE IS LIFE.
LIFE IS FULL OF HOPE.

The retirement home residents moved their heads to the music. At the refrain, there was even one lady who got up to start dancing, which encouraged me. Then they applauded, and Mr. Boulfou quickly took back his CD. Phew! It was over, and I was relieved . . . almost moved, since all of these old people suddenly reminded me of the good times spent with Grandpa Joff and Grandma Ragny. I told myself that they'd surely be proud to see me doing such a good deed, and if that'd happened, Grandpa Joff would've slipped me a buck to "sweeten the deal," as he often says. . . . Yes, fine, OK, dear future human—but no pain, no gain! Long story short, just as I was telling myself I was awesome and all that worry was for nothing, we sat down to eat with everyone since it was nearly lunchtime. One of them asked me five times in a row when I would come back for vacation while calling me Jules the whole time. We colored, made pasta necklaces, and played with Play-Doh.

As we were leaving, the residents gave us little bags with balloons and soft caramels. I kept the candy and gave the balloons to Lisa.

Saturday

It's fall break. <u>I'm in bed, sick.</u> I couldn't take the train to go to Brittany to see Grandpa Joff and Grandma Ragny. It's all because I didn't wear my coat last week. . . . 😞 So my mom bought me a big down jacket that's too long—I can't even walk when it's zipped up, it's so long. On top of that, it has <u>FUR</u> around the hood. You can be certain that when I go back to school, Raoul is going to call me a mama's boy. Dear future human, I'll write more to you later, because right now I have a fever and I'm starting to hallucinate.

MAX FASHION QUEEN!

Sunday

Dear future human,

It figures—just when I was finally able to go to Grandpa Joff and Grandma Ragny's house on vacation, I forgot my notebook. I hope that my parents (or even worse, Marion!) didn't find it while I was gone. 😔 I'd hidden it so well under my bed that I forgot all about it. Also, since I'm so clever, I wrote a warning in the front—which you must've seen. It'll discourage more than one person, I tell you!

THERE'S NO WAY ANYONE IS PUTTING THEIR NOSE IN MY STUFF!

In the end, it was an awesome vacation. Far from Raoul the Tool, his gang of idiots, PE, and all that crappy school stuff. The only downside was that I wasn't allowed to bring my Xbox. 😠

🙂 I guess it's OK, though, 'cause we're never bored with Grandpa Joff and Grandma Ragny, anyway. I said "we" because Lisa came with me. On the train I had to listen to Ben Didji the entire way. Lisa stuffed one of her earphones in my ear. Only at one point, everyone was staring at us . . . the headphones had yanked out of my phone and Ben Didji was shrieking throughout the entire train car.

Marion decided to stay home and hang out with her friends . . . and take more selfies, no doubt. I went fishing almost every day with Grandpa. I  love to breathe the ocean air, and since I'd been sick, Grandma said the salty breeze was good for my health. Grandpa always wants me to come fishing with him.

But as soon as we get set up, he doesn't let me touch the lines. So I just play with the worms, which ends up irritating Grandpa Joff because I lose them in the sand.

Lisa and Grandma made cakes
and knitted the entire time. Lisa
was determined to make a scarf. I
encouraged her (to keep the peace),
but the result wasn't all she'd
hoped for: 🙁 ————————→

Grandma and Grandpa also took
us to the cemetery, because it was
All Saints' Day, a day to celebrate
the dead. It was the first time I'd
actually been in a cemetery. We put
flowers on Aunt Simone's grave. I saw a big
tear roll down Grandma Ragny's cheek. 🙁 It
was at that moment that Lisa disappeared. It took
us a good half hour to find her; she was sitting in
front of pots of chrysanthemums, picking flowers to
make a bouquet for Grandma Ragny.
While I was looking for her, I passed
by a few old, broken, half-open tombs.
No one must have been taking care of them
anymore. They were really dark inside.

64

It made me think of *Zombieland*, my video game.  I was afraid a skeleton or something like that would crawl out of the hole. Since this whole thing had made me a little sad, at the end of the trip I went to a souvenir shop and bought key chains with the names of my parents and Marion.

The good news is that I found out the fur on my new down coat is removable. I took it off and, for some reason, left it on my bed. Later, I heard Grandma screaming in my room. When we came to see what was going on, she was hitting the fur with a broom.

Scram, you dirty animal!

BAM!
BAM!
BAM!

Tuesday

Dear future human,

I'll spare you the details about the return to school, because there's something MUCH MORE important:

🙂 **Zombieland 2** is coming out for Christmas! ,·,

Yeah, I saw the commercial on TV! So as far as Christmas gifts are concerned, I need to make sure my game is under the tree. 😝 I figured this was a good time to ask my parents for a little raise in my allowance. First I just wanted to bring it up with my dad. We understand each other when it's just us guys. But when Dad came home from work, he was in a terrible mood: his Russian clients canceled an order for one thousand sinks. 😬

A low blow for S Inc.

I wanted to broach the subject at dinner, but Marion beat me to it. She has to be telepathic . . . it's not possible . . . I'm missing something! But when my dad started doing conversions in rubles, I let it go.

Friday

Dear future human,

This morning while thinking about this whole allowance thing, I told my dad that we needed to spend more time together. I suggested that he come pick me up from school and then we could go wash the car together. 🙂 At CarClean, I began washing the rims with a little brush. Up to this point, everything was going great. Then my dad moved the car forward to go up on the rollers. I was waving my arms to guide him. Then he got out of the car before the big machine started up. We watched the car disappear into the tunnel. I suddenly realized that I'd left my window half-open . . . 😟 but it was too late—the inside of the car was soaked! But the worst part was that my backpack was sitting in the back seat. And when the dryers started, I saw all of my homework papers flying around the inside of the car.

TOTAL DISASTER! 😣

To top it off, I watched in horror as the math test Mr. Tamisole had returned to us that morning became stuck to the back window.

Monday

Dear future human,

After this incident, I permanently abandoned the idea of asking my dad for a raise in my allowance. However, I just thought of the PERFECT idea for my Christmas gifts this year: I'm going to collect coupons! Nonchalantly, I went to see my dad and told him I'd get the mail every day through December. JACKPOT! He said yes right away. I started my collection with a couple that weren't too shabby.

10€
AT FIXIT ALL*
*valid only on nails

25% off
all makeup at
SMELLGOOD

Wednesday

I just realized something: the month of December isn't the best time to collect coupons. Of course! 😑 You think "marketing" folks are stupid? They know that, unless we do away with Christmas, people are obligated to buy something this month.

Result: if I just stick with my own mailbox, I won't get very far. So, I decided to go door-to-door to the neighbors and offer to do little jobs in exchange for coupons.

So, I established a plan: 😊

MONDAY
Mrs. Quinion→bring in her mail

TUESDAY
Miss Roudan→walk her dog

WEDNESDAY
Mr. <u>Lopez</u>→buy his bread

THURSDAY
Mrs. <u>Martin</u>→scrape her windshield

FRIDAY
Mr. <u>Lupus</u>→prune his hedge

SATURDAY and SUNDAY → (rest.)

 Hey, hey! Don't you think my intelligence is extremely evolved for my century?

Today, Mr. Lupus gave me a coupon that's worth more than gold: a scratch card to possibly win a trip to a winter resort!

LET DOWN YOUR HAIR. FEEL THE WINTER AIR!

TRY YOUR LUCK. SCRATCH HERE!

Thursday

Dear future human,

Today, the principal brought us all into the auditorium to talk about <u>Operation Rice Bowl</u> for next week. It's a fundraiser for kids around the world who don't have enough to eat. 🙁

He explained how it works: we all have to bring in a bag of rice and drop it off in the cafeteria. The Friday before winter break, we're only going to be allowed one bowl of rice to eat in the lunchroom. The money saved on lunch will be used to buy food for underprivileged children or for orphans. If we're really generous, we can also bring in canned food, boxes of pasta, or other "nonperishable" food to send to the children.

I thought this was a nice idea, especially since Célia and Naïs are in charge of keeping the list of collected food items.

Friday

Dear future human,

I dropped off my bag of golden rice in the cafeteria and a huge can of fruit in the collection box (my favorite kind, on top of that—with the maraschino cherries). Go figure that Enzo Danleau's mom sent a note to the office that day saying that Enzo would eat "at home" next Friday because he is allergic to rice. . . .

Could I do Operation French Fries instead?

Dear future human,

Tuesday

 Oh man! What a night!

I came home from school
with Tom, and we were
in a hurry because I had to
walk Rocky, Miss Roudan's dog.
Tom said he'd come with me. You
should know that Miss Roudan's dog had an
accident two years ago when a car ran over his
back legs. Since then, he has only three legs,
and he limps. But he's still got to have
exercise to stay healthy, so that's why he needs
to be walked often. Since I have the keys, I
went to Miss Roudan's house, I found Rocky, I
put on his leash, and we went out for a stroll.
But after about ten minutes we ran into Naïs
and Célia.

79

I was showing off a little with Rocky—like, "Look how good I am with animals." Ladies love animals. Then I tied his leash to a post because the girls wanted me to look at the list of items for Operation Rice Bowl with them. I made sure they knew the bag of golden rice and the canned fruit WITH candied cherries were from me. I was showing off again because ladies love generous guys like me. They left, and when I turned around, Rocky was gone.

Tom and I looked EVERYWHERE, but there was no trace of him. Still, with his three paws he couldn't have gotten too far. There was only one thing we could do: make posters. Tom and I booked it to my house and started drawing pictures of Rocky. The sketch wasn't very flattering, but it would work.

 I took some tape and hung up our posters everywhere—except for the route Miss Roudan usually takes to get home.

But after almost an hour, it was obvious the posters weren't doing much.

Suddenly, Tom thought of something else: "What about the Japanese restaurant? I had heard a rumor that Japanese people apparently eat dogs!"

I grabbed Tom by his jacket and we bolted. As luck would have it, he was right! <u>They had Rocky.</u> They'd found him outside their door and were waiting for someone to claim him. . . . But, OK, I couldn't shake the image of Rocky inside a sushi roll.

I brought him back to Miss Roudan at the exact moment she got home. While I was doing that, Tom was taking down all of our posters. To show my gratitude, I gave him the scratch card to win a trip to a winter resort. . . .

Tom and I went through the secret passage today, and we saw that the graffiti had changed yet again. It was weird—it said:

Between finding Rocky at the Japanese restaurant and Operation Rice Bowl, I'm beginning to ask myself some questions. . . .

Dear future human,

Operation Rice Bowl was today. We all went to the lunchroom—except Enzo Danleau. He was crying when his mom came to pick him up at lunch, because I think he really wanted to participate. In the cafeteria line they served us a big plate of rice, and the principal rattled off an ENDLESS speech on generosity. Célia and Naïs were organizing the last of the donations in boxes. Naïs is so pretty. But that moron Lucas Saillard—you know, one of Raoul's three goons—had stashed a chocolate bar in his coat pocket. He wanted to seem cool in front of Raoul and the two others, but his plan backfired. Raoul immediately went to tell on him.

Evidently, at that very moment, Célia and Naïs were standing next to the principal to give him the list of donations. In front of the girls, Raoul started bragging about how "loyal" he was to report those who weren't "working for the greater good." As for me, I think there's nothing worse than betraying your friends.

December (23)

Dear future human,

Ta-da! I am pleased to inform you that my collection of coupons is officially complete:

10€ AT FIXIT ALL*
*valid only on nails

—for my dad

25% off all makeup at SMELLGOOD

—for my mom

A SECRET CODE for private sales at COOLTHREADZ

—for Marion

A card with EMERGENCY PHONE NUMBERS

—for Lisa

1 ticket to win a 32-VOLUME encyclopedia set

—for Tom

1 day of discount prices at GARDEN STUFF

—for Grandpa Joff and Grandma Ragny

Lisa wanted to help out—she thought my idea was great. We wrapped everything and put names on all the presents. It's gonna be a huge hit!

Dear future human,

My plan didn't turn out <u>AT ALL</u> like I'd hoped. Since we put the named gift tags on the presents AFTER we'd wrapped them all, everything got mixed up. What do you think happened?

Grandma Ragny
A card with EMERGENCY PHONE NUMBERS

Mom
10€ at FIXIT ALL*
*valid only on nails

Dad
25% off all makeup at SMELLGOOD

Grandpa Joff
A SECRET CODE for private sales at COOLTHREADZ

Marion
1 ticket to win a 32-VOLUME encyclopedia set

Tom
1 day of discount prices at GARDEN STUFF

Lisa
NOTHING

The cherry on top all of this was that Lisa thought my idea was SO great that she wanted to do the same thing. Except she's only eight years old, and she isn't exactly great at picking out gifts for people yet. So that means we all found ourselves with coupons for a <u>free quote for roof restoration</u>, a <u>reduction on tree pruning</u>, a <u>complimentary property estimate</u>, a <u>trip to a mosque</u>, and even a <u>guided visit of a funeral home</u>.

The whole thing completely fell apart. As for me, I guess it could have been worse. Marion gave me her eight-color pen, even though I haven't wanted it for about three years.

Merry Christmas! This gets rid of it!

In Grandpa Joff and Grandma Ragny's
present I found a big mouse head and a
long body split down the middle with a zipper.
They explained that it was a pair of pajamas.
Grandma Ragny told me she bought it
at the store and that, if I wanted to, I
could exchange it for the hippopotamus version.
When people say that age eleven is when kids
become ungrateful, I CAN CONFIRM! I had only
one more present to unwrap—the one from my
parents—and in it I found . . .

Zombieland 2

I called Tom right away and asked him to come
over and play my shiny new game. He told me that
his parents had scratched the ticket for the trip
to the winter resort . . . and they won!

89

Monday

Dear future human,

Here I am back at school, and it's starting off GREAT! Mr. Schmitt announced that in April "pen pals" from England are going to visit us here in France. Each one of us will host a student for a week, but beforehand we're going to write each other via email during technology class with Mrs. Boulauche. Since Mr. Schmitt wants to show off his "perfect" students, he came up with a new rule. When he enters the classroom, now we have to stand up. And when he says:

 —GOOD MORNING, CLASS!

We have to respond:

—GOOD MORNING, TEACHER!

If you ask me, it's pretty lame.

Dear future human,

I've been back in school for a week, and I can officially inform you that the gymnastics unit is over. Boy, am I happy! Now it's time for the pool unit with Mr. Ramoupoulos. I have to say, I'm rather gifted in the art of swimming, 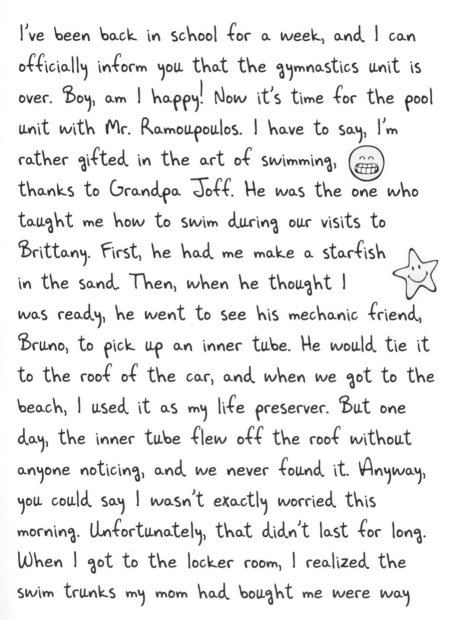 thanks to Grandpa Joff. He was the one who taught me how to swim during our visits to Brittany. First, he had me make a starfish in the sand. Then, when he thought I was ready, he went to see his mechanic friend, Bruno, to pick up an inner tube. He would tie it to the roof of the car, and when we got to the beach, I used it as my life preserver. But one day, the inner tube flew off the roof without anyone noticing, and we never found it. Anyway, you could say I wasn't exactly worried this morning. Unfortunately, that didn't last for long. When I got to the locker room, I realized the swim trunks my mom had bought me were way too small. I guess it was sort of my fault because I hadn't felt like trying them on in the store.

It took three good attempts to get my swim cap on, and I nearly lost an eye and caused some premature balding in the process.

I don't know why, but public pools are always cold and scary. They must add some strange concoction to the chlorine or something like that, because when you breathe, it immediately gives you a panic attack!

But I think it was even <u>WORSE</u> for Enzo Danleau. His mom tried to get him a medical exemption, but no luck— his doctor was a strong proponent of sports and wasn't hearing any of it. So, to encourage him, Enzo's mom had bought him a swimsuit with *Baywatch* written on it. To be honest, Enzo looked pretty sharp in his swim trunks, but the poor guy's teeth were chattering, and he was shaking so much that he slipped into the footbath.

Enzo, watch out!

Dear future human, the footbath is the stupidest invention ever. You're supposed to dip your feet into it to clean them before you enter the pool water, but really every species of bacteria in the entire world is just splashing around inside it.

At least that's what I thought. . . . I didn't want to put my feet in there, not until Mr. Ramoupoulos pushed me in and explained that the footbath contains a disinfectant that actually kills the germs.

After that, Mr. Ramoupoulos was waiting for us, sitting on the edge of the pool. He blew his whistle and then introduced us to David, our swimming coach—a mountain of muscles with an enormous neck and a tiny little mustache.

He spoke loudly, informing the class that we were going to take a swimming test that would separate us into groups by skill level. I told myself that I'd start slow, not showing what I was capable of right away. In the shallow end, I pretended not to be able to swim. I flailed my arms and legs around wildly and spat water. I was placed in the blue group—the one staying in the shallow end—with Enzo Danleau. Tom found himself in the yellow group, for average swimmers, and Raoul Kador was in the red group. For a second I relaxed. Then all of a sudden, Enzo inexplicably started sinking . . . even though he could touch the bottom. Courageous as I am, I didn't hesitate to help him.

I'm familiar with the rescue hold, because last year Marion got her lifeguard certification and she practiced on me. I dived to the bottom and grabbed Enzo under the arms. I

then heroically brought him up with all of my strength, and I swam back to the steps with him in tow. For a minute it felt like I was in a TV show: tropical ambience, sunset, palm trees, and plenty of girls admiring my bravery. Just as I was hoping Naïs hadn't missed A SECOND of my rescue, suddenly I heard Mr. Ramoupoulos's deadly whistle. From the edge of the deep end, he gestured for me to join the red group.

When I woke up this morning and painfully dragged myself to the bathroom, I looked in the mirror and saw that I had an enormous zit on my nose . . . right in the middle! Absolutely hideous . . . I'm positive I caught this thing at the pool. Dear future human, I hope that in your time, researchers have successfully modified human DNA to permanently remove the "acne" gene that's been ruining my life for the past few months. I dug around in my mom's makeup bag and stumbled upon a tube full of beige cover-up cream—which I was sure would save the day. I put a little on my nose, spread it around, and then checked in the mirror. It worked! It was hardly visible. I left for school. Tom wasn't at our meeting spot, so I sent him a text.

And on the wall of the secret passage, there were red swim trunks drawn with "S.O.S." written underneath. . . . It reminded me of Enzo Danleau's pair. Strange. The mysterious graffiti artist couldn't actually be Enzo, could it?

With Tom being absent and still no explanation for the perplexing graffiti . . . the day wasn't off to a great start. All day long, I had the feeling that everyone was looking at me funny, staring at my nose. Some people, like Rami Nouch, were totally fixated on it. Well, Rami Nouch is nearsighted, and he's squinting half the time, so that doesn't really count. Anyway, I told myself it was all in my head and that I just had to stop thinking about my pimple, especially since it was well hidden under my mom's cover-up cream. But in the middle of Mrs. Boulet's French class, I heard people whispering my name. I started wondering why Lucas Saillard kept chuckling and calling me "Tigger."

I pretended not to hear or let it bother me . . . but when I got home, the miserable reality was blindingly obvious, especially when Marion busted out laughing upon seeing me. . . .

 SHE'S SO ANNOYYYYYING!

I ran into the bathroom and saw in the mirror that, on my pimple and all around it, I had a HUGE dark orange mark. In fact, it was far worse than this morning!  I searched in my mom's bag to find the tube of cover-up, and this time I actually read what was written on it. . . .

SELF-TANNING
CREAM

Saturday

Today was Lisa's ninth birthday. She invited six friends over, and my parents hadn't prepared <u>ANYTHING!</u> I think they totally forgot. Parents are so weird, always coming unglued over nothing. In this case, it was two hours before the party, and my parents were arguing because they couldn't find a plastic tablecloth. They have a whole box of them in the basement. . . . And so they STILL weren't getting anything done. 😕

Thankfully, I saw that they were completely out of it and took matters into my own hands— I didn't have much else to do anyhow. I must admit—I'm quite good in desperate situations. 😁 I saw there were still several expired yogurts in the fridge to make a cake with, there was banana-guava-pomegranate juice that NO ONE wanted, and there was a lot of candy that Lisa had gotten from her friends' birthday parties.

I first gathered everyone up, and then I suggested to my parents that we go to the fast-food place on the corner and steal balloons. (Stealing free balloons, that works!)

Between the five of us, we got ten balloons. Even Marion told me I saved the day.

As for presents, I came to the rescue on that too. Lisa loves pretending to have serious injuries. She dreams of one day breaking an arm or a leg. In her free time, she empties boxes of bandages and puts them on together to "make a cast." The other day when I was at the pharmacy with my mom, I spotted a big display of walking canes for the elderly. I went back to the store without telling anyone and bought one. Dear future human, you have to admit that this time I proved my TREMENDOUS generosity. I spent most of my pocket money on it, but the idea was so wonderful I couldn't resist. Afterward, I even thought that this gift could be useful for Grandpa Joff or Grandma Ragny one day too.

When Lisa unwrapped her gift, she squealed: "Cool! A cane! Awesome!" My parents stared at me in amazement. They were so proud of me and my brilliant find! All of her friends were jealous, and they kept arguing over who was going to try the cane first. That gave me another idea—yes, I know my imagination is boundless 😉—and I organized a big cane race. In the end, the girls didn't want to leave—they were clinging to me and yelling my name. Future human, my first fan club was born! 😊

This day is one for the record books. . . . There's no doubt about it; success is addicting. I think I was born to be famous!

Wednesday

Dear future human,

I have to tell you some totally awesome news! (Obviously, I'm on a lucky streak right now.) Tom's mom called tonight to ask if I wanted to go skiing with them during our next break. Remember? Around Christmas, the neighbor, Mr. Lupus, had given me a scratch-off ticket to win a trip to a ski resort. Then, after the incident with Rocky (Miss Roudan's dog) that almost ended in tragedy, I gave the ticket to Tom. And the parents of that old slug <u>won the trip!</u> I was a little jealous at the time, but everything worked out after all since the trip is for four and Tom is an only child—so I get to go with them! I am SUPER happy: I've never skied before, and now I can get out of another trip to Brittany, which has started to become deadly boring lately!

Monday

Dear future human,

This morning in computer class, Mrs. Boulauche organized a "videoconference" with our English pen pals . . . so that we could "introduce ourselves." To be honest, no one really wanted to stare right into the teacher's webcam. And she was <u>livid</u> that everyone was pushing and shoving each other, trying not to be in front. No one was getting into the camera view, and Damien Chico was putting up bunny ears behind Lucas. It was at that exact moment Mr. Schmitt came in to bring a little order to the class, making us do his lame routine:

Good Morning, Class. Good Morning, Teacher. . . .

☹️ . . . Even though it was the middle of the afternoon. We calmed down, and suddenly the English class appeared on the screen. The kids seemed nice but a little nervous. 😕

We all lined up one after another to say, "Hello! My name is Max. Nice to meet you." The only issue was that Titouan had a cold: "Hello! By dame is Didouan. Nice to beet diou." Which sounded like he said, "Nice to beat you." When the video call was over and Mr. Schmitt left, Mrs. Boulauche showed us pictures of the English middle school. Then she projected photos of the students on the wall, along with each one's name.

Obviously, despite the teacher's disapproval, we all were laughing and whistling at Penny's irresistible beauty, Michael's ENORMOUS nerd glasses, and Brian's florescent-yellow, glow-in-the-dark shirt he was wearing in his picture. But the worst was when this boy named Conrad appeared.

MULLET

GRANDMA'S WOOL SWEATER

It's weird—I didn't remember him from the video meeting. The entire class started laughing—even me—and I crossed my fingers that Conrad would be Raoul's pen pal. Since I was having such a streak of good luck, anything was possible. Then Mrs. Boulauche pulled up a chart that matched our photos with those of our future pen pals. This all-knowing graphic was going to tell us which student we would be paired with. . . .

And that's when the drama started—what a disaster!

 NOOOOOO!

I even saw Célia and Naïs burst out laughing. Double noooooo! 🙁 Why did I get Conrad? But worst of all: Raoul didn't get a BOY pen pal; he got a GIRL pen pal! This was so unfair! And it just gave him another reason to show off.

RAUL IS SO ANNOYYYYYYING!!!!!
Even more than Marion!

LIST OF THE <u>WORST</u> THINGS THAT COULD HAPPEN TO RAOUL KADOR

DESSERT IS SERVED

— Have him eat Rocky's turds instead of chocolate mousse in the cafeteria

— Make him do MY homework FOR LIFE

— Cut his hair while he's sleeping

— Transform him into BROCCOLI

Suck out his brain with : diabolical machine

— Make him run ten laps around the stadium NAKED like Jérémy (Oops! I said it again!)

113

114

Dear future human,

This pen pal deal is killing me.
I am DIS-GUST-ED.

What if Conrad smells bad, or he's only interested in science or quadratic equations, or he plays the flute—or worse—he's a psychopath or a serial killer? I don't feel so good. I looked at photos of ex-convicts on my dad's computer, and I feel like Conrad has the exact same face. And

what if something happens to me while I'm asleep? And Conrad runs away in the middle of the night? No one would ever know what happened to me. Just to be safe, I made a sketch of him for police reference.

At home, my mom could tell something was wrong. Last night, she came to my room to find out what was up. I explained everything to her. 😠 She told me not to worry, that we shouldn't "judge a book by its cover," and that Conrad was undoubtedly very nice. To cheer me up, she also said that she'd "maybe" take me to AllSports to buy me a ski suit. So I laid it on thick, and then we went there later. 😊

I came out of there with a sweet ski outfit with a photo of Pietro on the front pocket. Awesome! If I hadn't had this issue with the pen pal, I would've had to wear Marion or Lisa's old ski suit. . . . 😝

kiddie size

On the other hand, my mom told me to put the fur lining back on the hood of my winter coat in order to stay warm on the ski slopes. I didn't have the courage to tell her it bit the dust during fall break at Grandpa Joff and Grandma Ragny's.

Dear future human,

During computer class we're exchanging emails with the English kids so we can get to know them a bit better before they arrive in April. Mrs. Boulauche asked us to introduce ourselves, talk about our family, and share our "hobbies" . . . or at least our interests.

Conrad is thirteen years old, and he also has a sister that he "haaaaaates!" I told him how to say that in French. At least we have one thing in common.

At the end of class last week, Mrs. Boulauche had also asked us to prepare a presentation on a monument in Paris, using text and photos. I chose the big Ferris wheel at the Place de la Concorde, because I'd gone there with my parents for Marion's twelfth birthday. Well, actually, at the last minute Lisa was scared and began screaming. 😱 Since she couldn't stay at the bottom alone because she was too young, and since it was "Miss Annoyyyyying's" birthday, Marion made me stay and watch Lisa. So, technically, I didn't really ride the big Ferris wheel, but I was officially there. 😬

That idiot Raoul stole a college thesis on the Eiffel Tower off the Internet and shot it to Alison, his pen pal. He wanted to act all smart, but the document ended up with Mr. Smith, our pen pals' French teacher, who sent a few words to Mrs. Boulauche.

You will write six double-sided pages for me on the history of Gustave Eiffel, his inventions, and the World Exposition of 1889.

Raoul was called to the principal's office, and they threw the book at him.

Vengeance!
It was the best day of my life.

Anyway, there's only a few days left until break, and I'm going to the mountains with Tom. I am SO psyched to leave this gang of losers and forget about this whole pen pal thing for a little bit. I need some fresh air!

On my way home, I passed by the secret passage and saw that there was something new written on the wall:

I'd heard this expression before, because Marion and my mom use it to refer to "that time of the month." It was still really odd! Neither Mom nor Marion could be behind all this graffiti. . . .

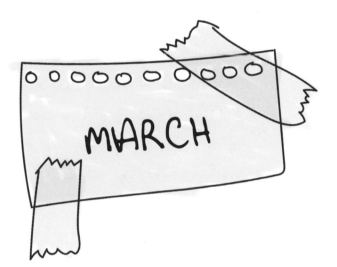

Sunday

I'm back from the ski resort!

Dear future human, I decided to leave my notebook at home. It was <u>TOO risky</u>! Imagine if Tom had found it during our trip. . . . He would have found my thrilling, visionary stories and stolen my ideas! (◕‿◕) That wimp would've double-crossed me, which would've ruined my chances of becoming the super-magnificent witness of my time. (◡‿◡) The vacation was awesome . . . except that there was practically no snow and I almost died several different times. (◡﹏◡) We stayed at a little ski resort, which was at an elevation too low to have enough snow. So, instead, Tom's parents made us go on a lot of hikes.

It was cool, but the ground was covered in black ice, so we had to take little steps to avoid falling flat on our faces every three hundred feet. Let's just say it was fun for about the first ten minutes, but then it always went on for two hours. . . . 😤 We also went to a skating rink. I'd never been ice-skating in my life, and neither had Tom. We hung on to the side and moved around in circles like ants, laughing the whole time. We pretended we were walking on ice like the living dead in *Zombieland 2*. 🙂

Except at one point I started to think I was finally getting the hang of it. I told Tom that I was going to attempt a triple axel. I knew exactly what to do, because I'd watched the figure-skating world championships at Grandpa Joff and Grandma Ragny's house, but . . . I fell miserably and bruised my tailbone. So that meant Tom's mom had to put ointment on my butt every night . . . s embarrassing! 😖 I made Tom promise to NEVER tell anyone about it, even if he was tortured.

Other than that we ate raclette and fondue, blueberry pies, and some weird stuff like beef-tongue sausages and cow-udder cutlet. At night, we played *Zombieland 2* and talked a lot about who could be writing on the wall of the secret passage. . . . Well, I guess it was mostly me talkin since I'm starting to think it's suspicious. At first, we laughed about it, and I thought that it was just a coincidence, but, for some time now I've had the strange feeling that the wall KNOWS EVERYTHING—that it's TALKING TO ME! 😨

I insisted we compare theories on who was doing the writing:

Mr. ~~Schmitt~~→No, too lame.

(Raoul Kador)→Hmm . . . maybe! 🙂

~~Rocky~~→No, he has only three paws, he can't run, and, also, he's a dog.

~~Enzo Danteau~~→No, he's too much of a sissy to risk getting caught!

Rami Nouch→No, his handwriting is terrible.

~~Jeremy~~→No, he didn't come back to school this year.

(Naïs)→Hmm . . . why not? 🙂

CONCLUSION OF OUR ANALYSIS:
MAXIMUM alert!

We have to keep a close eye on everyone in our class, our school, and even the city. From now on, we won't miss any clues.

The last day of the ski vacation there was finally snow. Tom and I made a gigantic snowman, and his parents took us skiing. There was no way on earth I was getting past the bunny slope. It's too bad, since being a naturally gifted skier would have certainly impressed Naïs. But to be honest I was just happy to be able to go back home and say I'd skied 😆 Of course, it didn't all go like I'd wanted it to. On the ski lift I dropped a pole. I saw it fall—a long way down 😅 —and it landed in a totally deserted non-skiable zone. Then I had to wait for Tom's mom to find me another one. On top of that I had trouble holding on to the T-bar of the ski lift.

Then, a fellow passenger made an announcement over the ski lift's loudspeaker: "Who's in charge of this boy currently keeping the other skiers from getting to the slope?" Total humiliation!
The one time that I got it right, I was so happy that I neglected to see the little snow mound waiting for me at the end of the lift. I got my foot stuck in it when I was trying to get off and ended up turning myself into a ridiculous rolling snowball.

The last night there, Tom's parents took us out for dinner. We had sausages and French fries. Everyone had a great time, and afterward the hotel hosted a karaoke night. Dear future human, I swear the idea didn't sound appealing, especially not when the host DJ called my name to have me come up and sing. That scoundrel Tom sold me out! At first, I didn't want to go up there, but Tom really wanted to join me—so we sang "Hope and Life." It was the only song we could think of! I didn't expect it, but everyone applauded wildly. In short, we had a great night: it was fun to be together as a family and to get to know Tom's parents better. I also realized I missed my family too. So before leaving this morning, I went and bought a few souvenirs for my parents and sisters.

I bought wooden mushroom-shaped salt and pepper shakers 😜 (with "100% mountain pine guaranteed, made in China" written on them), a pencil holder in the shape of a snow boot for Lisa, and a cup with a deer on it for Marion. 🙂

😠 Tomorrow I have to go back to school, and my mom just sent me a text:

Maxie-poo, I see the light on under your door. Go to bed!

APRIL

Tuesday

Dear future human,

Today is April 1, and do you know what that means in my day and age?

APRIL FOOLS' DAY!

And, believe me, today I woke up with an absolutely brilliant plan. At school, we have an old coin-operated telephone booth. Yeah, I know what you're thinking: a real antique! But guess what—these things are totally solid, and the one in our school is still ticking. One time I went to take all of the change that was stuck in the coin return . . . and there was a small fortune in there! I sent Tom a text.

HEY U OLE SLUG! BRING UR PIGGYBANK 2 SCHOOL

OK!

What's cool about Tom is that he never really says no and he doesn't ask too many questions. I found him in the secret passage and explained my plan: during recess, we were going to make prank calls to people on the payphone.

In the morning when the bell rang, Tom and I ran to the old phone booth, which was hidden in a little courtyard where no one ever goes. We picked up the phone, put in the coins, and dialed a random number. This guy answered, "Hello?" and with a very confident and adult voice I said:

—"Hello, Sir, are you familiar with the game show *The Price Is Right*?"

Jackpot! He watched it every day! I immediately went into game-show mode. Tom whispered responses to me:

—"What a wonderful coincidence! We're going to be taping several shows in your area, and you were selected at random to play with us and possibly w a multifunction kitchen mixer. Are you ready?"

The guy was totally ready.

—"Do you know the exact price for a Hershey's chocolate bar?"

The guy was deep in thought. I encouraged him:

—"Go on, Sir, venture a guess?"

Tom and I were dying laughing. The guy was convinced he was going to win something.

—"Uhhh . . . 3.90€?" the guy said.

—"Bingo! The price is right! You are the proud winner of a superb kitchen mixer. So, what will you cook with your new appliance?"

I must have ad-libbed a bit too much, and the gu started stuttering in the receiver. It was time to hang up.

—"Dear Sir, please hold, and our receptionist will take your address in order to send your gift. Congratulations from everyone aaaat . . . *The Price Is Riiiiiiiiiiight!*"

 I hung up! Tom and I were doubled over laughing.

Then he wanted to make the next call. I think my comedic talents and powers of persuasion impressed him. We emptied our pockets and put the coins in the payphone. Tom dialed. A lady answered and bam! We told her to pack her bags, because she'd won a trip to a tropical paradise! Then the bell rang, and we hung up fast and returned to class.

After that, things went downhill.

The principal showed up right in the middle of Mrs. Grumot's chemistry class. He looked furious.

Apparently, the payphone hadn't stopped ringing for the last two hours. The secretary in the office ended up answering, and she found a lady on the other end. The lady was so insistent that the secretary had to

By the way, exactly how many people is the trip for?

call the principal to explain to the woman that she'd dialed the wrong number, that this was a middle school, and that his "establishment" had absolutely nothing to do with VACATION packages. Apparently, the lady was really, really disappointed, and she started crying into the phone. She'd announced the good news to her husband and the entire family, because it'd been over ten years since they'd gone on a vacation more than thirty miles from their house.

All of a sudden, I felt completely guilty. It was just a silly idea, and I didn't think it would have such dramatic consequences for this family. In the back of my head, I heard a voice whisper that we needed to find a way to fix our mistake. I shot a look at Tom, who pretended not to see me.

Then the principal demanded:

"The students responsible for this tasteless joke must turn themselves in by the end of the day or you will all be forbidden from attending the big party for the English pen pals at the end of their stay."

That was the punishment for our class, but I'm sure the principal had loads more in his head for the entire school. . . .

The bell rang, and as soon as we left the classroom, I went over to Tom. I realized that this old slug had dialed a cell phone number! Huge mistake—everyone knows it's way easier to trace a call from a cell phone. 😠 We hesitated to turn ourselves in, since this party could be THE ONLY CHANCE IN MY LIFE to get closer to Naïs and maybe even ask her to dance. 😍

I wound up convincing Tom to go see the principal with me.

We explained to him that we'd made the calls because Mrs. Boulet, the French teacher, had advised us to improve our dramatic skills, which was a total lie. The principal grumbled an endless lecture—like usual—on the importance of respect, values, and "all that jazz," as my dad would say. Then he wanted us to call the lady back and apologize. He had written her number down on a slip of paper but couldn't find it. Our lucky break! He'd lost it. We escaped with only a note for our parents and a paper to write on the question, "Does too much joking kill the fun?"

As I was leaving, I noticed a piece of paper on the ground. On it was written the woman's number. I picked it up discreetly and put it in my pocket. On the way home, this stupid joke and the poor family deprived of vacations kept running through my mind.

When I got home, I looked up her address and pulled the shoebox out of my closet to take stock of my savings. There wasn't much left since I bought the cane for Lisa. . . . 😖 Then I got an envelope ready, put all of my money inside, added a note, and I left to go mail the package.

THE SOHOOL AND I WOULD LIKE TO APOLOGIZE FOR THIS STUPID TELEPHONE PRANK.

SINCERELY, THE PRINCIPAL.

Wednesday

This morning a guy came and took away the phone booth. . . . 🙁

Monday

Dear future human,

The students from England arrived last night and . . . Conrad was with them. (He's sleeping right now, so I'm taking the opportunity to tell you about the first day.)

Mr. Schmitt and Mrs. Boulauche had told us to meet in the parking lot of the local stadium and stressed that we all had to be <u>ON TIME</u>. But we ended up waiting for the bus for two hours. The English class was coming from Hastings, in the south of England. They'd spent eight hours marinating in two buses and one boat, and let's just say they weren't smelling fresh when they arrived. Mr. Schmitt welcomed them, and then after talking with Mr. Smith they started dividing up the students.

CÉLIA with PENNY

ENZO with GARRY

LUCAS with MICHAEL

~~RUSSEL~~ with ALISON

NAÏS with DIANA

RIAMI with BRIAN

DAMIEN with ROBERT

MATHIS with WARREN

TITOUAN with RILEY

LOUISON with JANE

MAX with CONRAD

TOM with WILSON

EMMA with KIM

LISE with TRACY

Conrad was a lot bigger than I'd imagined, and at first—from the front—it looked like he'd cut his hair . . . but it was actually in a ponytail! Each pen pal took his or her bag, and each one of us took our partner. 😝

When Conrad got to my house, I brought him to my room and tried to start a conversation. But I have to admit, my average in English is close to a D, and I'm pretty sure his French wasn't any better.

This your lit and this is *le mien.*   What?

This is the *salle de bains,* please, take a *douche* every day.

C'est quoi une <u>bathroom?</u>

Please, open your book.

What is your favorite color?

Then he unpacked his stuff—I'd been considerate enough to give him a little space in my dresser—and he pulled some little jars of homemade jelly from his bag. 😕. He gave one to me and then went to pass out the others to the rest of the family. I was afraid that dinner was going to be an epic failure, but fortunately, once we sat down, my dad monopolized all of the conversation. He thought it was a good opportunity to practice his English. 😬

Do you want some fromaiiiiidge?

Tuesday

I slept horribly last night. Since Conrad 🙁
was coming, my mom and dad went to AllSports
to buy an inflatable mattress, like one for camping.
That thing made a terrible racket every time
Conrad turned over. It squeaked so much that I
dreamt there was a pig in my room.

We found Tom and Wilson in the secret
passage and went to school. The inscription "The
Redcoats are coming" was still there—nothing had
changed. Tom explained to them that it was a
kind of "welcome sign," made by the city's famous
anonymous graffiti artist. 😁 Wilson and Conrad
seemed really impressed. Raoul wanted to bring
Alison on his bike, but because of the weight of
two people, his chain came off and they had to
finish on foot. Conrad came with me to my classes
all day long. In the beginning, he wouldn't let me
out of his sight. 🙁 Clingier than an orangutan.
He wouldn't stop talking to me and asking all
sorts of questions about the school:

"Where is the *cantine?*" and "Where is your class?" and "Mrs. Boulauche, it's a funny name, isn't it?" and "Do you have a *stylo* for me?" and "The weather is too bad," and blah blah blah . . . all of it in English, in a totally <u>INCOMPREHENSIBLE</u> accent.

Frankly, he didn't really try to make himself understood, and that put the pressure on me! I ended up finding tricks to avoid him: I stayed locked in the bathroom stall for all of recess; during lunch I sat at the first table with only one seat left; and during biology, when we had to team up with our pen pals to dissect a rabbit's foot that smelled like cheese, I ran to the nurse's office and declared that I was an active member of the AARDA (Albino Angora Rabbit Defense Association) and that I was abstaining from participating in such a slaughter.

I think Conrad took his role as a pen PAL a little bit too much to heart. But at home I was stuck. . . .

I'm going to ask him to play *Zombieland 2* to pass the time.

Wednesday

Today Mr. Schmitt and Mrs. Boulauche took us to see the Eiffel Tower. As soon as we got there, Mr. Schmitt wanted to flip a coin to decide whether we were going to take the stairs or the elevator. Louison Toinou said "tails" for the elevator, and it fell on heads. . . . 😖 On top of that, in order to impress the English kids, Mr. Schmitt had chosen tickets for the <u>very top.</u>

. . . I honestly thought Enzo Danleau was going to kick the bucket. He kept puffing on his inhaler every twenty steps, and he was as red as a tomato. 🙁 Conrad DID NOT stop taking pictures: the Eiffel Tower as seen from below, as seen from above, zoomed in on the bolts, the view from the top, the view from the bottom. He even took a selfie. Raoul acted like a hotshot in front of Alison. Damien Chico and the idiots were also showing off in front of Diana, Naïs's pen pal. They kept bowing in front of her and yelling, "Your Majesty, Your Majesty." 😊

151

But Raoul didn't appreciate the fact that they were trying to one-up his "flirting" schemes. So he tripped Damien, who fell and almost ended up as flat as a crepe hundreds of feet below. Too bad for Raoul, since Mr. Schmitt wasn't far and noticed their little game. Raoul had to recite his six double-sided pages on the history of Mr. Eiffel and his inventions for the World Expo in 1889 that the principal assigned to him . . . all of it in English. Since he has a brain the size of a pea, that doesn't leave him a lot to work with.

Meester Eiffel mayke zi Eiffel Toweur een 1889 for zi Exposition Universelle . . .

Tom and I were really happy to be there—it was something different from the four walls of our middle school. Then we went back down and had a picnic in a park not far away. My mom had made us some supposedly "healthy and balanced" sandwiches . . . made with jelly and cucumbers. She must've been trying to make Conrad happy— or at least get rid of one of the little jars—but I have to say it was disgusting.

Conrad and I looked at each other, and we threw the sandwiches in the trash. Luckily, we had salt and vinegar chips . . . I have a serious weakness for salt and vinegar chips. Classes were already over by the time we got back to school.

Oh! Dear future human, I forgot to tell you that Conrad is crazy good at *Zombieland 2*! So I invited Tom and Wilson to come over and play a round. Conrad and Wilson showed us loads of tips and tricks to win more food, to get more lives, to avoid being bitten by the living dead, to build a fortress in case of a pandemic, and to take out zombies. We went from level three to level five in no time.

YES!!!!

😀 ·· Dear future human, **Saturday**

Sorry I've been gone for two whole days—I was making the most of them to play *Zombieland 2* with Conrad. It was an opportunity I couldn't miss! First, Conrad helped me get to level nine 😋 (my ultimate dream) and, second, my parents left us totally alone because they were convinced that my "friendship" with Conrad was beneficial for my English. 😁 On the other hand, I think that the only phrase Conrad learned in French is "I demolished you, old slug!"

Tonight: TOTAL PROPAGANDA! ·;·

We found out the so-called party organized by the middle school for the English pen pals is nothing but a little "get-together"! 😠 I should have known. Teachers are first-class con artists! Dear future human, one thing's for sure: they'll never get me to turn myself in to the principal again for a simple get-together.

Evidently, Enzo Danleau wasn't allowed to go out that late, because Garry came by himself. At first I thought it was fun to be at school on a Saturday night, but Mr. Schmitt, Mr. Smith, and Mrs. Boulauche couldn't come up with anything better for us to do than have a "garbage garb" competition. It's this totally ridiculous game where you get into teams and the teachers give you big trash bags filled with recycled junk: empty cans, egg containers, toilet paper, tape, etc. Each team has to create a costume for one of its randomly assigned members and then parade him or her in front of a jury. . . . I found myself on a team with Naïs and Diana, Louison and Jane, Emma and Kim, and Lise and Tracy. Basically, except for Conrad, I was the only boy on my team. Still, guess which sucker was picked to be dressed up? Well, duh, ME! 😖 On the other teams Titouan, Rami, Wilson, and . . . Raoul were the lucky ones chosen for trash duty. 😁

As soon as Mr. Schmitt gave the signal, I found myself surrounded by a hoard of overexcited girls who, in less than five seconds, had already slipped a trash bag over me (of course making sure they didn't suffocate me while putting my head inside)! Then they decorated my head with toilet paper. They made all sorts of things, like bracelets with paper towel rolls that they glued together. . . . Conrad couldn't do anything to protect me; he was forced to pass them scissors, glue, and anything they needed to make me look ridiculous. Naïs was laughing the most. . . . I didn't know what to make of that. 🙁 Anyway, I was totally stuck. Once finished, they all seemed pleased with the result.

When I turned around, I could finally see what everyone else looked like!

RAOUL AS A KNIGHT

TITOUAN AS A HOMELESS GUY

WILSON AS A MONK

RAMI AS A VAMPIRE

Rami pretended to chase the other students and bite them, but because he's such a klutz, he tripped on his trash bag cape and had to end his night in the emergency room.

☹ Raoul was apparently really proud of his costume, especially since it was a lot less ridiculous than mine. But Wilson's costume was by ✌😁 far the best! He won the "garbage garb" contest hands down. Then we snacked on what everyone had brought. The principal came "expressly" to give a never-ending speech thanking the English students for coming and telling them how we would all be "exceedingly delighted" to come and see them in England next year. 😠 Then my dad came to get Conrad and me. Evidently, when I got home,

I was still wearing the trash bag, and, of course, in the hallway I passed Marion, who exploded with laughter. ☹

MAX IS GARBAGE!

Conrad and I escaped to my room. I was fuming. This evening was a total disaster; I made an absolute fool of myself in front of Naïs, and Marion—SHE'S SO ANNOYYYYYING! Conrad could see that things were not going well, so he told me that his big sister was even more "boooooring!" Then he went to the kitchen and came back with another big trash bag. He cut out a hole and put it on like me. Then he started jumping on the squeaky mattress and yelling, "boooooring!" "boooooring!" "boooooring!" I did the same—it blew off some steam, and we had a good laugh! Conrad heads back home tomorrow morning. We promised to send each other texts and emails. I won't go as far as to say that I'll miss him, but it wasn't half as bad as I'd imagined.

Dear future human,

For the last ten days I have been on spring break, but guess what? We couldn't go to Grandpa Joff and Grandma Ragny's this year for the simple reason that they decided to "treat themselves" to a "little vacation" to Africa . . . no big deal!

And to think that I was the one who was beginning to find our vacations in Brittany boring!

Instead we stayed home. After the whole unfortunate incident with my math homework sticking to the inside of the car windshield (and after my last report card), my parents had decided to make me do some extra work to "catch up." One night my mom came home from the lab with a (surprise.)

MATH GOALS:
THE VACATION
WORKBOOK
FOR
PROS!

I thought that she'd brought me a book of Pietro stickers, because I saw the word "goal" on the cover, but no!

Luckily, I found out that all of the answers were in the back of the book. I jumped right into it, making sure to show my intense focus, and finished the workbook in two days . . . and my mom didn't suspect a thing.

Wednesday

Dear future human,

To be honest, school has felt empty since Conrad and all the other pen pals left. It's back to painful reality for me.

> I have a NEW problem to solve, and it's enormous!

After the dance night turned out to be just a little "get-together," Raoul Kador decided to spare no expense and set things straight. This morning he gathered the entire class in the courtyard to tell everyone he was organizing a HUGE PARTY at his house at the end of June. Well, at least you could say his announcement wasn't last-minute. . . .

"DEAREST MORONS, I WOULD LIKE TO DO YOU THE HONOR OF INVITING YOU TO MY PARTY ON SATURDAY, JUNE 21!"

But this was another one of his nasty stunts. 😠
Basically, he told us that all of the girls were
<u>automatically invited</u> but that us boys had to take
a series of tests to have <u>THE RIGHT</u> to come.
Then he took out a large paper with all of the
trials, and I realized it wasn't going to be a piece
of cake.

Raoul explained that, because he was "so
generous," he was going to give us at least two
weeks to practice, so we could stack all the odds
in our favor to complete the tasks and come to his
party. Dear future human, you must think I'm pretty
pathetic—and under normal circumstances you'd be
right. Ordinarily, I would never allow myself to be
reduced to such blackmail . . . but Naïs will be
there! 😳 I'd already missed my chance to get
closer to her at the "big party" with the English
students. No way I'd miss this one too.

First party + Naïs = Guaranteed super night

Also, I don't think I really have a choice. 😕

165

DAMIEN —> CARRY A BALL OF BREADCRUMBS IN HIS
BELLY BUTTON FOR THREE HUNDRED FEET.

MATHIS —> STICK A BOOGER ON HIS MATH HOMEWORK.

LUCAS —> YAWN REALLY LOUD DURING
COMPUTER CLASS.

ENZO —> KISS LOUISON TOINOU ON THE MOUTH.

RIAMI —> GO TO THE BLACKBOARD AND BREAK ALL
THE CHALK IN FRONT OF MRS. BOULET.

TITOUAN —> DRINK A MOUTHFUL OF WATER FROM THE
POOL FOOTBATH.

ILIESS —> PUT OIL ON MR. BOULFOU'S CHAIR.

ANGELO —> LET OUT A HUGE BURP IN FRONT OF MR.
SCHMITT.

RAPHAËL —> SHOW UP LATE TO CLASS FOR AN ENTIRE
WEEK AND GIVE RIDICULOUS EXCUSES.

NOAH —> EAT A WORM.

JULES —> HAVE A STARING CONTEST WITH MRS.
GRUMOT DURING THE ENTIRE
HOUR OF CLASS.

TOM —> RUN THREE LAPS AROUND THE ENTIRE
PLAYGROUD WITH HIS SHOELACES TIED
TOGETHER.

MAX —> WALK AROUND ALL DAY WITH TOILET
PAPER STICKING OUT OF HIS PANTS.

In the middle of Mrs. Boulet's class, Raoul Kador passed me a note to give to Célia to give to Naïs. Just my luck—Mrs. Boulet caught me and took the piece of paper. Then she read it to the entire class. 😶

> NAÏS, WOULD YOU LIKE TO SLOW DANCE WITH ME?   YES ☐   NO ☐ 😊

The class howled with laughter. 😣 I wasn't just roasted; I was burnt to a crisp. In the hallway, Raoul and his clique made little hearts with their fingers at me. Raoul is really starting to tick me off, and I don't want to take his stupid test. . . . 😡 Suddenly, Tom had a brilliant idea. He remembered this old TV show, *Hypnotik*. People in the audience let themselves be hypnotized by this guy who waved all sorts of talismans under their noses while really intense music played in the background.

Max + Naïs

It seemed to really work, because apparently this guy made people do everything: eat grasshoppers, imitate a pig rolling in mud . . . and he only had to snap his fingers for the people to wake up. One time, though, Tom heard on the news that a guy was hypnotized at home in front of his television as he watched the show. His wife, his kids, and the emergency services all tried to wake him—but they couldn't. The next day, he disappeared into the woods. An entire search party went looking for him, but the guy was <u>nowhere</u> to be found. Then the news went on to something else, and we never learned what happened to him.

And so the great idea is:

WE HAVE TO FIND A WAY TO HYPNOTIZE RAOUL!

With a little luck, no one will be able to wake him up, and he'll disappear into the woods <u>FOREVER</u>. Either way, Tom and I were game to give it a try. We had nothing left to lose.

Wednesday

This morning when Tom and I were going to school, we passed by the secret passage and HYPNOTIK was written on the wall. . . . We were completely freaked out. 😮 Tom quickly pulled me away toward the library, because we were on a mission: become professional hypnotists and get rid of Raoul. We only found a workbook with exercises for self-hypnosis. But at least it was a start. 😁

We went home, and I started by practicing on Tom. It was really technical! You had to do personality tests, take an "introspective" quiz. . . . Pfff! What a pain. 😤 Then we went and typed "hypnosis session" in my dad's computer, but what we found on the Internet wasn't at all like TV. For starters, there wasn't a video—just a static image of a black-and-white spiral with totally depressing music playing in the background. The hypnotist, who had a terrible Southern accent, told us to hold out our hands and bring them closer and closer together as if they were magnetic.

At first we tried to play along, but the  "video" lasted over a half an hour. We turned it off and went to sleep.

Then I woke up to Tom calling me Pietro, like my favorite football player. He was begging me for an autograph and wanted to take a selfie with me. I thought that the hypnosis worked on him, and I was <u>totally spooked.</u>

Tom busted up laughing! He really got me good. We had to admit, despite our best efforts in this new hobby, neither one of us was experienced enough to hypnotize Raoul. We were forced to make a radical decision: give up on hypnosis, which clearly required a certain amount of expertise. We were really running out of time.

. . .

Wednesday

Dear future human,

Besides Tom and me, no one talked about Raoul's party at school. I think that all of the boys were trying to downplay the whole ordeal to avoid the tests. But this morning the big idiot reminded us of the "basic rules" of what he'd decided to call "Raoul's Grand Slam Party." There he goes again with his smug mouth! He told us again that we could complete the tasks whenever we wanted, but he had to be there to witness and give the green light. That put pressure on everyone, and the tests started up this morning.

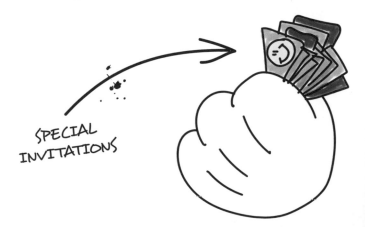

SPECIAL
INVITATIONS

In the middle of computer class, Lucas started yawning extremely loudly. 😪 Raoul immediately gave Lucas an invitation, but Lucas also earned a note for his parents about how "alarmingly" tired he was. Iliess also came out OK. Since he didn't have any oil, he put an <u>entire bottle</u> of glue on Mr. Boulfou's chair in social studies class. 😄 The teacher didn't notice anything, but when the bell rang, we saw he couldn't get up. He tried pulling on his chair, and then he told us to leave. Afterward we saw the principal going back and forth between his office and the classroom. He finally went to the classroom with the lost and found bucket, and Mr. Boulfou came out wearing red sweatpants that were way too short for him. . . . 😁 Iliess passed with flying colors and was given special congratulations from Raoul, along with his invitation.

Thursday

Lucas's and Iliess's achievements encouraged Damien Chico and Mathis Balma. . . . Evidently, Raoul witnessed the booger stuck on the math homework that was turned in to Mr. Tamisole yesterday. We all protested because we didn't see anything, but Raoul told us he'd seen it and his approval was what mattered. Today after lunch, Damien was able to carry some bread in his belly button for three hundred feet. 😄 He should have lost it during the last fifty feet. He just barely caught it at the last minute, and Raoul clarified that the purpose of the test was not to let the bread fall on the ground— so Damien had earned his invitation. Raoul is playing "favorites"! 😠

Dear future human,

The tests continue, and I don't see how I can get out of this mess. Rami broke all of Mrs. Boulet's chalk, and since he's cross-eyed, the teacher even comforted him because of his "handicap"! In Mr. Schmitt's class, Angelo let out a trumpeting belch during the middle of singing "God Save the Queen." On the playground, Raoul and Noah didn't find any worms, so Noah gulped down five ants. And at the swimming pool, Titouan even swallowed a mouthful of water from the footbath. I was so disgusted.

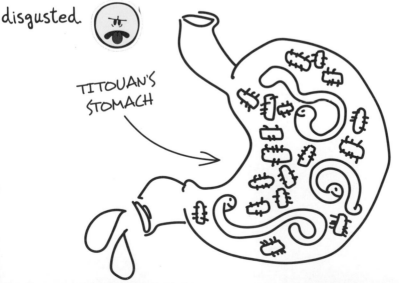

TITOUAN'S STOMACH

175

Wednesday

At recess this morning <u>Enzo Danleau gave it a go</u> . . . with Rami's help. Rami was in charge of "kidnapping" Louison Toinou in the little courtyard area where the phone booth used to be, the place where no one ever goes. Raoul was hiding, and Enzo was waiting to kiss her. But actually, according to what we heard, Louison spotted Raoul first. She threw herself at him and planted an enormous kiss right on his mouth. And Enzo was immediately eliminated. And now, Louison has been following Raoul everywhere.

In other news, Raphaël's been late to class for the last three days. On Monday, he claimed he'd been chased by a lion that had escaped from the zoo. On Tuesday, he said that he had amnesia and didn't know where he was. And this morning, he told us that he had to go back home because he'd forgotten his right hand, which is his writing hand . . .

Thursday and Friday, Raphaël kept coming in late and inventing all sorts of excuses: that he had fallen in a manhole and then that he had to go to the emergency room because he had a fingernail growing out of his left ear. Raoul agreed that Raphaël had "qualified" to go to his party, and Mr. Tamisole—the math teacher—said that Raphaël had earned himself a two-hour detention on Saturday morning.

Apparently on Saturday morning this idiot Raphaël kept going with the joke; he showed up late claiming he was sucked up into a vacuum cleaner. He then had to stay in detention for two more hours.

Thursday

By this morning, only Jules, Tom, and I were left to take our tests—and Raoul was pressuring us even more.

Jules asked Raoul for a "special exception" to take his test during art with Miss Trinfon, because he was failing Mrs. Grumot's chemistry class. Raoul, "in his great generosity," agreed. But this was a bad move on Jules's part, because when we got to class, Mrs. Trinfon told us we were having a pop quiz. The test was to make a portrait of a caterpillar using India ink. The model, frozen in a jar filled with chloroform, was sitting on a stool near her desk. Jules had to choose: either stare at Miss Trinfon for the whole hour and fail the test or focus on the worm he was supposed to draw! But a good grade in art was the only way Jules would make it to seventh grade, so he had to give up Raoul's challenge.

This is it! Today was the last day to pass Raoul's tests—my LAST chance to be able to go to Raoul's party and hang out with Naïs. It was terrible. This morning I found Tom at the secret passage, and somebody had drawn a big earthworm on the wall. The "artwork" was signed, Hypnotik. The mysterious graffiti artist now had an alias: <u>the same name as the hypnosis TV show!</u> Tom told me he thought it was really strange and that, as soon as we were done with sixth grade, we should absolutely clear up this mystery over the summer. Then we had to mentally prepare ourselves for the tasks that awaited us at school, especially me, because spending the entire day with toilet paper coming out of your pants isn't exactly a walk in the

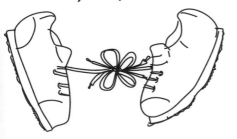

park! Tom had put on his laced sneakers, and we went off to school.

Raoul was waiting for me with a roll of toilet
paper that he'd been nice enough to bring from
home. He'd even . . . personalized it. Like a
prisoner sentenced to death, I pulled off a big
piece and stuffed the end in my pants. The rest
of it hung pathetically behind me.

But the events of the last few weeks took
a drastic turn during recess. For a third time,
Raoul gathered the whole class and even called
over some of the other kids in our grade to help
in the last test—Tom's.

I was anxious to finish these stupid tests. And believe me, future human, as soon as Tom tied his laces together and stepped up to the starting line, I promised myself that I would spend the entire summer break learning hypnosis, sorcery, and other dark arts in order to KO Raoul and any other future enemies that might come my way. 😠 Tom set off with a hobble. Everyone was encouraging him, and I think that at that moment my buddy Tom let the exhilaration get to his head—at exactly 171.78 feet, he crashed to the ground with a terrible scream. We all gathered around Tom, who was in bad shape. 😵 My survival instincts took over. I moved the crowd back and made eye contact with Naïs, who was staring at me, very impressed—I'm almost certain of it. 😍

I asked her to go get help right away. I knelt down next to Tom and held his head.

It reminded me of scenes from the war movies I watch with Grandpa Joff. I looked for something to wipe off his forehead with, but all I could find was the toilet paper with "Raoul Party" on it.  Then I saw Tom's knee, and trust me, future human, it was not a pretty sight. I heard Tom trying to whisper something into my ear.

Max,
I have something
to tell you. . . .

But before he could say anything, the principal came hurtling over, and everything happened so fast. He told me to move back, but I refused, telling him that Tom was my best friend and abandoning him was out of the question. When I turned my head back toward Tom, I realized that old slug had blacked out! The ambulance arrived five minutes later. Tom was taken to the emergency room, and the diagnosis was grim: "femur double fracture and one month in a cast"! Holy cow, it was serious! The vibe at school wasn't the same for the rest of the day. Nobody dared to say anything. And just before the last swimming class with Mr. Ramoupoulos, I was called to the principal's office. He demanded that I tell him the whole story, promising anything I said would stay anonymous and that I "shouldn't fear any retaliation." I gave him a blank stare, I thought about all of the horrible stuff Raoul Kador and his gang of jerks made us go through, and . . .

I spilled the beans!

At the end of the day, Mr. Schmitt asked me to bring Tom his backpack and write down all of the homework in his planner.

HOLY GUACAMOLE! SON OF A MUSKET! This morning I opened Tom's planner . . . and nearly died from SHOCK!

The pages were scribbled with notes and drawings, the same ones from the secret passage! The mysterious graffiti artist, Hypnotik, was TOM? The same person who made invisible ink out of yogurt and raced snails? To think that he had me from the beginning! How did I miss it? I don't know if I can ever get over this. That old slug won't get out of it that easy. . . . How could he keep something like that from his best friend? This was practically high treason. So, I decided to bring Tom's stuff over and confront him pronto. But when I found him at home, he was still in a lot of pain. And when I gave him his planner, his eyes opened wide, then he closed them

187

and tried the old pretend-to-be-passed-out trick. There was a long silence before he finally reopened his eyes and confessed everything. Tom was definitely the graffiti artist. He had seen something on TV about a famous street artist who wrote rebellious messages on walls. He told me that, since he was shy, it'd given him the idea to express himself without anyone knowing it was him. He also said he was hoping to be famous someday. I busted up laughing 😄 and told him about my notebook for subsequent generations, the one you're holding in your hands, dear future human. I said that I too would become famous someday. We spat on our hands, shook them, and promised to never tell anyone about any of this! And to increase the value of my notebook, I asked him to give me an autograph! 😉

Dear future human,

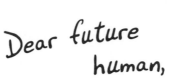

I have two things to tell you: one good and one great! 😄 After the whole test ordeal and Tom's accident, Raoul's parents were called in to meet with the principal. The result: <u>Raoul is in trouble, and his party is CANCELED!</u> But the best part is that I asked my parents if we could have the party at our house. I hesitated initially because I was a little scared they'd say no. But I talked to Tom about it, and, yesterday morning, I saw on the wall of the secret passage: "Go for it, Max!" So I gathered the courage and asked my parents. At first, they were totally freaked out. I should mention that Marion's last sleepover didn't end so well. She'd invited five friends over, and they wanted to play a game of musical sleeping bags. That meant walking and jumping around the sleeping bags while music played. When the music stopped, everyone had to jump into one. Except that at one point the police rang the doorbell, responding to a "nighttime disturbance." Mr. Lopez, our neighbor, had filed a noise complaint. The police had to call my parents, who were out for dinner, to get them to come back on the double. But with ALL the work I put into bringing up my English and PE grades, and for finishing sixth grade strong, they said YES! 😁

It is my first party and, believe me, I'm going big!

I sent a text to everyone in my class. 😜

RIAOUL'S PIARTY MOVED TO MIAX'S HOUSE! EVERYBODY'S WELCOME!

Everyone said yes right away—except for Naïs, who took two days to accept the invite and in the process managed to put me in a constant state of anxiety. 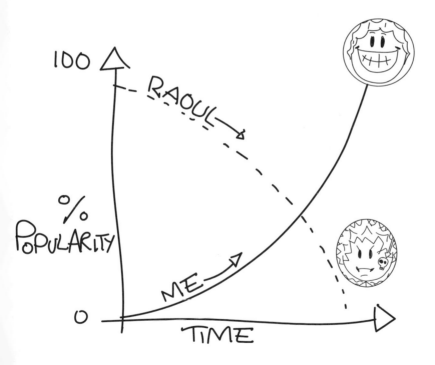 Still, I think my brilliant idea to move the party to my house will totally raise my popularity at school.

Friday

After class, I went by to see Tom at his house. He'd just come back from the hospital, and the doctors had given him a lighter cast and some crutches. That meant he could come to my party! 😀 Then my mom took me to FiestaGalore to buy decorations. She really tried to give me the piñata we'd forgotten to use for Lisa's ninth birthday, but when she saw my face, 😠 she realized it wasn't worth pushing. We also went to the supermarket to get some drinks and salt and vinegar chips. And guess what? Marion even offered to take care of the music. I told her she could—but no tricks, OK? 😉

My plan was going off without a hitch when
suddenly I started feeling REALLY guilty. . . .
🙁 <u>What about Raoul?</u> I imagined him all
alone in his room Saturday night while the rest
of the class was having a total blast at my
house. Was that really what I wanted—me, Max,
the bighearted person and genius of the future?
I sent him a text:

I went and asked my mom to try to convince Raoul's parents. I was sure that she'd find just the right words so that they'd let him come. She thought that my request to include him was very generous. 🙂 Apparently, Raoul's mom is really involved with school. In elementary school she chaperoned all of the field trips, she managed the booths at the fundraiser, and she organized the annual school carnival. This year, in sixth grade, she ran the Reading Passion club, a group that was "deeply appreciated" by the principal. 😬 My mom told her on the phone that she was sure the party would be a good opportunity for Raoul to make amends with his class . . . and she volunteered to help with one of the reading sessions in exchange for Raoul's participation in my party.

😉

Saturday night . . . late

☺

The party was a total success! Tom came a little early to help me blow up balloons. Then everyone else showed up. Even Enzo Danleau was there, although my mom called his mom three times to reassure her that everything would be OK. Naïs and Célia came a little late. Naïs was pretty, even with her new poufy hairstyle. 😍 Raoul Kador arrived last. After about five minutes, he called for silence. His parents had made him write an apology speech to us, which he droned on about like the school principal.

😠 "Dear Dorks,
OK, this year I gave you guys a hard time, but it's only because I'm so much cooler than you. Anyway, I'm sorry for my attitude this year, and thanks, Max, for inviting me! I'm still not sure his party's going to be as great as the one I would have hosted at my house. Just you guys wait for next year. Have a great summer, everyone!"

Marion put the music on. At one point in the night, Damien Chico wanted to propose a dare. I thought, "Not another one—that bites!" But actually, it was a game. The idea: one girl and one guy had to slow dance with each end of a licorice rope in their mouths. They had to nibble at the candy until they kissed. Louison rushed over to Raoul and invited him to dance, Tom went over to Célia—hopping on one leg— and . . . me? I held out my hand like a perfect gentleman to Naïs. I was afraid I was about to be totally ignored, but she accepted! Marion put on a slow song, and we started dancing with the licorice between our teeth. My heart was beating out of my chest, but I was able to keep my cool. I'd almost eaten half of the rope, and I closed my eyes to kiss Naïs.

😬 But all of a sudden, the song was interrupted by the voice of Ben Didji screeching out across the room. When I opened my eyes, I saw that Lisa had replaced Marion, who was off sending a text to her friends. 😲 It was all messed up again, but this time I had the feeling there was something between Naïs and me.

At the end of the night, everyone signed Tom's cast before leaving. And that old slug promised me that he'd kissed Célia, but I don't believe him for a minute. 😊

Sunday

Dear future human,

Sixth grade is over. And if I look back on it, I think I can say that my first year in middle school ended on a HIGH NOTE, despite all the obstacles. Tom and I made it through, and, best of all, next year we won't be the little twerps anymore! Tom and I had a great idea. (You must be thinking, "Again?!") We decided to take an old shoebox, fill it with all of our memories of this year, and bury it behind the wall in the secret passage—in the vacant lot.

We wrapped the box in plastic bags, and as soon as we added the last shovelful of dirt on top, Tom and I were both a little sad. 😢 So, we decided to dig it up at the end of seventh grade and replace it with a box of memories from that year. Isn't that a <u>GREAT</u> idea? 😁

Dear future human, I'm sure that you'll be able to put all of your mementos in a hermetically sealed space capsule. . . . But until then, see you next year!

Andrews McMeel Publishing
a division of Andrews McMeel Universal
1130 Walnut Street, Kansas City, Missouri 64106

www.andrewsmcmeel.com

18 19 20 21 22 SDB 10 9 8 7 6 5 4 3 2 1
ISBN: 978-1-4494-8987-8
Library of Congress Control Number: 2017950784

Made by:
Shenzhen Donnelley Printing Company Ltd.
Address and location of manufacture:
No. 47, Wuhe Nan Road, Bantian Ind. Zone,
Shenzhen, China, 518129
1st Printing—1/8/18

Editor: Jean Z. Lucas
Illustrator: Timothy Alan Jones
Art Director: Diane Marsh
Production Manager: Chuck Harper
Production Editor: Kevin Kotur

ATTENTION: SCHOOLS AND BUSINESSES
Andrews McMeel books are available at quantity discounts
with bulk purchase for educational, business, or sales
promotional use. For information, please e-mail the Andrews
McMeel Publishing Special Sales Department:
specialsales@amuniversal.com.